ELYSIUM

ELYSIUM

GEOFF WOODHOUSE

Matador
Unit E2 Airfield Business Park,
Harrison Road, Market Harborough,
Leicestershire. LE16 7UL
Tel: 0116 2792299
Email: books@troubador.co.uk
Web: www.troubador.co.uk/matador
Twitter: @matadorbooks

ISBN 978 1803132 747

British Library Cataloguing in Publication Data.
A catalogue record for this book is available from the British Library.

Printed and bound in Great Britain by 4edge Limited
Typeset in 11pt Minion Pro by Troubador Publishing Ltd, Leicester, UK

Matador is an imprint of Troubador Publishing Ltd

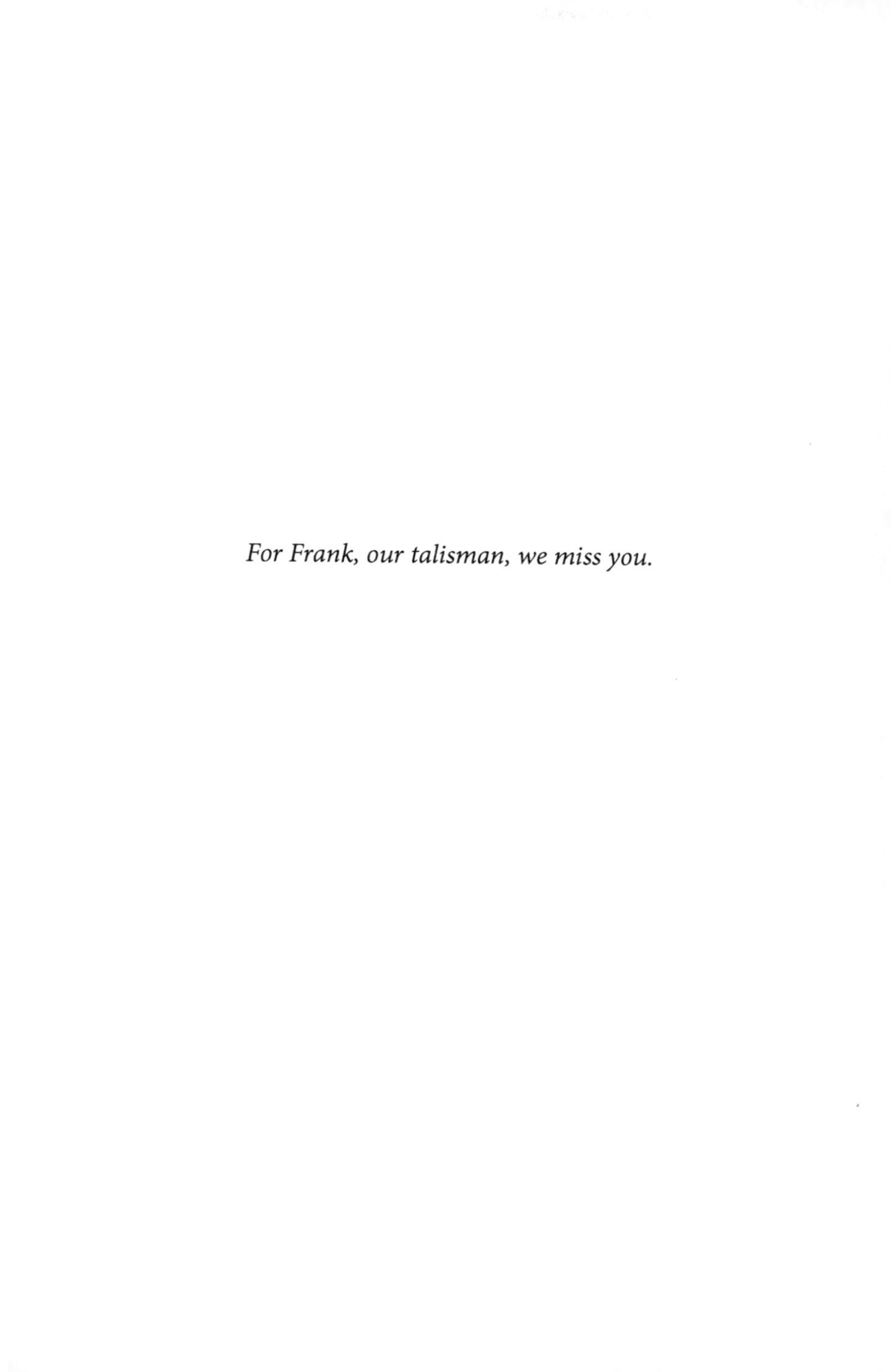

For Frank, our talisman, we miss you.

CHAPTER ONE
CAPTAIN STEPHENSON

I fell in love with *Elysium* before she was born, when I was shown the naval architect's drawings in the bright, open-plan studio which served as the headquarters of Elysium Liner Corporation in Miami. With sixteen decks and standing at roughly the same height as the Arc de Triomphe, and a quarter the length of the Champs-Élysées, she would be one of the largest cruise ships in the world. I felt like a child opening the box of a prized Meccano set as I took in every detail of her elegance and engineering wonders. "She will upstage the film stars and supermodels who sail on her, yet she will be capable of navigating the rigours of the Southern Ocean," I was assured by Lars Karstadt, the Swedish designer who led the project. "Each one of the 120 luxury residences will be fitted out to the individual specifications of its owner," he proudly told me. "We have one owner who wants us to recreate the cabins of his superyacht, sourcing the fittings from his yacht builder." I had long since ceased to be surprised by the passions of the global elite and told him, "I guess that's what you would expect if you are going to spend upwards of $10 million on a new home."

I was in Miami to meet Lars and the *Elysium* team, to agree terms for my appointment as *Elysium*'s first captain and discuss candidates for our deck and engineering officers. Like everything to do with *Elysium*, it was also a marketing opportunity, including interviews and video clips designed to sell the remaining luxury residences. Public relations are a core skill for a cruise ship captain, and I always get a buzz in front of the camera. The interviews were filmed on the pool deck of the Brickell Hotel, overlooking Biscayne Bay, and hosted by French models, Catherine Solange and Richard Rouseau. Elysium took over the whole pool deck, and it felt like I was an interloper in a fashion show. Catherine introduced me. "Captain Stephenson, you have spent your whole life at sea, twenty years as a first officer and cruise ship captain in the Mediterranean, the Caribbean and the Indian Ocean. Tell me about some of your favourite moments at sea."

I knew the question was coming and had thought about my answer, designed to appeal to our target audience of the global elite. "For me a perfect cruise is a luxury voyage of discovery. I want our residents and their guests to experience the exhilaration that I feel when we visit iconic ports like Hong Kong, when we explore the outstanding natural beauty of the Great Barrier Reef or the Norwegian fjords, when we conquer the Northwest Passage, when we retrace the steps of the great explorers to Petra or Chichen Itza."

I explained to Richard that, "Unlike a conventional cruise ship, *Elysium* will be a residential cruise ship for ultra-high-net-worth residents, each buying a luxury apartment and a stake in the owning company. The residents are essentially buying into a lifestyle, designed to stimulate the mind, body and soul. They get to choose our itinerary, which could take them to the grand prix or tennis in Monte Carlo, Singapore and Melbourne, world heritage sites like Halong Bay, the imperial palaces of China or the old city of Dubrovnik. We are looking to attract a relatively young family demographic, with an inspiring programme of water sports, personal training and wellness."

The *Elysium* was my last big project in a life which has brought me the highs and lows of our profession. I was proud of the fact that my personal journey took me from the tenement blocks of Glasgow, where I was raised by my illiterate, alcoholic mother, to the bridge of the *Elysium*. I never really planned a life at sea, I just fell into it when my uncle begged a place for me at a spartan maritime academy. I guess that I had an incentive to excel, since the only real alternative for me was a career in the services. Travelling the world on a cruise ship struck me as much more fun than being on the wrong end of an Exocet missile in the South Atlantic. And so it proved. By twenty-five I had cruised the Caribbean and the Mediterranean; I had tasted the nightlife of Barcelona, Dubrovnik, Lisbon and Rome. I had fallen in love in Santorini and San Juan. Maybe it was the fear of what I had left behind in the tenements of Glasgow that made me work my way through the deck ranks until I became a first officer at thirty-five and captain at forty. Each posting gave me the opportunity to start afresh, effectively wiping the slate clean and jettisoning the baggage which had accumulated with the last project. It is a nomadic existence. Thank God I never married, since it would have been impossible to be a faithful family man. In my twenties and thirties, I must have slept with one hundred women in one hundred ports, although never on board, and there was a certain sexual thrill about fleeing when it was time to return to ship. In my forties I would sometimes regret not having my life partner, but at sea you live for the moment and there is little time for contemplation. By my fifties, ready to start my last project on the *Elysium*, there were no regrets, since I was effectively married to my job.

My honeymoon was our maiden voyage, my rock star cruise, when the residents were joined by A-list celebrities from the worlds of fashion, film and music on a six-day cruise from Miami around the Caribbean. I milked my moment in the sun with the world's beautiful people, an odyssey of Instagram reels steaming out of Biscayne Bay, accompanied by a cacophony of ships' horns and fireworks. For six days and six nights I lived the dream, hosting cocktails, beach parties and open-air rock shows for the global elite. The real star of the show was *Elysium* herself, maybe not the largest or the fastest cruise ship in the world, but certainly the most beautiful.

Elysium's success is all about her exclusivity. The residents have to believe that they are buying into a black-card exclusive lifestyle, membership of which is by invitation only. It isn't just about money. Sure, you need to be able to find several million dollars to buy a residence, but you also need to be able to pass the country club test. Just like the members of an exclusive country club, you must be highly groomed, sassy and, above all, really interesting. I tried to meet all of our residents on our maiden cruise, and all of them passed the country club test with flying colours. At the A-Deck bar you could easily meet a private detective, a Hong Kong real estate entrepreneur, a Mexican stylist or a Grammy-award-winning artist.

I don't have the money to afford a residence on *Elysium*, but I can certainly entertain our residents at the A-Deck bar, and I would like to think that most of them would count me as a friend, even though I am much older than all of them. Social barriers evaporate after a few weeks at sea, and I get to know many of our residents much more deeply than my own mother.

I often wonder what she would make of me now. I deeply regret not staying closer to her during my adult life. In truth there was always an easy excuse. I could never get home for Christmas since I never had shore leave. I couldn't write to her since she couldn't read, and I couldn't call her whilst we were at sea. I only managed a few snatched calls when we were in port, and even those were a chore. She died in her early fifties, having led a wretched and loveless life.

The sea was my escape from the toxic shades of grey in Glasgow. It brought colour to my monochrome world. It was like replacing a black-and-white television set with high-definition colour. No matter that as a young man I slept in a bunk which I shared with an arrogant redneck on alternate watch. No matter that our quarters were airless, cramped and stank like stale beer. No matter that every relationship was transitory. I lived for my pride in a job I loved, the thrill of arrival at an iconic port like Hong Kong, the sexual freedom of shore leave, the adrenalin rush of maritime exploration, the elegance of our ship and the natural beauty of our anchorage. As I matured and made my way up the ranks it was an increasingly comfortable existence, until I reached the pinnacle of the captain's suite on the *Elysium*, which boasted a double bedroom, ensuite bathroom, elegant saloon and a desk salvaged from the *Queen Henrietta*. Like a lot of professions, as you rise up the ranks you lose some camaraderie, some satisfaction of completing a particularly complicated navigation; you feel the weight of responsibility; you become a diplomat, man-manager, a host and a company man.

My journey to the captain's suite was not exactly smooth sailing. In my twenties and thirties, I was a party boy, spending my shore leave in the bars, clubs and brothels of the cruise ship circuit. As a good-looking guy with no commitments, I had a licence to party, and I took full advantage. Together with three or four mates from the ship, we would head into town to drink ourselves silly, then on to a late-night bar or club in search of girls. Most of the time we would pass out in some seedy club, unable to walk, let alone perform in bed. Sometimes the evening would end in feeble sex in a hotel room for rent by the hour. Sometimes I was sober enough to sleep with the loosest girl in the club; sometimes I got lucky and stayed with them a few days. One time in Athens I spent a whole weekend in bed with two American students. I became increasingly adventurous and was essentially addicted to sex.

Just before Christmas one year when we were moored in Gibraltar, I developed a hacking cough. I didn't think it was serious until I was engulfed by wave upon wave of symptoms, blood on my pillow, acute diarrhoea, raging night sweats and, most scarily, I was struggling to breathe. The ship's doctor checked me into hospital in Gibraltar, telling me, "I can't risk you going to sea – let's have everything checked out in Gibraltar and you can rejoin the ship at Cittavecchia."

He probably saved my life since, within twenty-four hours, I was in an isolation room on a drip with steroids and antibiotics pumping into my body and oxygen flowing into my lungs. I couldn't hold anything down and felt completely drained of energy. Over the next three days I endured needles and tubes, administered by a stream of medics, a nurse watching my vitals from outside the transparent tent surrounding my bed. My consultant, a fellow Glaswegian named Gordon who had found his way to Gibraltar, peppered me with questions. "Where have you visited in the last three months? Have you had unprotected sex? How much do you drink? Do you take recreational drugs? Have you slept rough?" On the fourth morning, my fever subsiding, Gordon arrived with six medical students in tow, cheerily telling me, "The good news is that you don't have tuberculosis, and we can release you onto a general ward. The bad news is that you have suffered pneumonia. It is subsiding, but you will need strong antibiotics and steroids for at least three days. You should recover, but you will remain weak for at least six weeks. We must find the underlying cause, since a thirty-nine-year-old man as fit as you should not get pneumonia. I want you to take a series of further tests. Do you think you are at risk of having HIV? Have you slept with men or prostitutes?"

The sound of the three letters 'HIV' sent shivers down my spine, but I thought it pretty unlikely. Yes, I had slept with many women, but I was always pretty careful. I didn't really sleep properly for several days, often waking up drenched in sweat. Maybe it was the orchestral coughing from my nameless fellow patients. Maybe it was the lingering doubt. I confessed to myself that I didn't really know what had happened in those drunken nights in Barcelona, Dubrovnik, Lisbon and Rome.

The test itself was easy, just one more needle in my arm. The forty-eight-hour wait for the result was agonising. Gordon told me the result himself. "I am afraid that you have tested positive."

The words spun around in my head – I felt dirty, disoriented and, above all, scared. "How long do I have? One year, two years, five years, ten years?"

His answer scared me rigid. "The truthful answer is I don't know. You have a high viral load, and your CD4 count is below two hundred. This means that we need to start anti-retroviral treatment straight away. We have some pretty good drugs now, but you will probably need to take them for the rest of your life."

I had a million questions, but I realised that I was at the start of a very long journey, and they could wait. Maria, the nurse who had spent so long at my bedside when I was inside the tent, came to see me. She instinctively knew the turmoil that was going on inside my head, even before I told her my test result. In a simple act of kindness which will live with me forever, she held my hand as we talked about life in the Caribbean, her birthplace, which I knew well from our Caribbean cruises.

Gordon referred me to an HIV specialist, Professor Gilligan, who gave me a much more upbeat assessment of my life chances. "If we start antiretroviral treatment immediately, and your body reacts as I anticipate, we can suppress the virus. There is no cure, but we should be able to keep the virus at bay. Once we have the virus under control, there should be no reason why your HIV status should change your life expectancy."

Physically, I was one of the lucky ones. Just as Professor Gilligan predicted, the antiretroviral drugs reduced my viral load to undetectable levels, and my CD4 count steadily began to rise. I had a few scares, like the moment when my skin turned yellow, a classic symptom of anaemia, which meant that I had to endure blood transfusions. At first, the drugs felt toxic; I felt weak and unsteady, developed rashes and fungal infections, and it took years for my body to stabilise. Eventually I reached the point where Gilligan was happy for me to move to six-monthly appointments, when he would take blood tests to check my viral load and CD4 count and review my medication. In my late forties, the treatments were so advanced that I could take just one pill daily, and there was no medical reason why HIV should affect my life.

Mentally and emotionally, it was a different story. In those early days I felt scared, unclean, excluded and stigmatised. I took a look around the waiting room at Gilligan's surgery and I was scared by the gaunt faces, the deathly stares. Gilligan had told me I was about to find out who were my real friends, and I felt sure that I would not be able to go to sea, get a mortgage, travel or take out health insurance. I told just one friend, and our relationship changed forever. On the surface, he was understanding, but I noticed that he was always careful not to drink from the same glass or use the same bathroom. He became dismissive and began to treat me like a child. So, I decided to keep it secret, telling only those people who really needed to know, like medics and sexual partners. I told myself that the company didn't need to know, provided that I was always careful. At first, I would go into a cold sweat at the mention of company health assessments, visa applications or insurance questionnaires, but eventually the world caught up with the fact that the risk of infection from anyone with an undetectable viral load is negligible. The stigma never goes away, but right now it is a social stigma, rather than a fear of catching a life-threatening disease.

I didn't rejoin the ship at Cittavecchia, but I did return to work three months later, and it was probably life at sea which gave me back my confidence and self-esteem. I eventually realised that I was still the same person, just unlucky. I am still careful, but I have conquered my fears.

CHAPTER TWO

JUAN

I have always thrived on being unconventional, so why should home ownership be any different from any other aspect of my life? I had made it to forty without ever having signed a tenancy agreement, let alone a lease, yet here I am, buying my first home, the most expensive penthouse on the world's most exclusive cruise ship.

I guess the apartment says everything about me. Drop-dead gorgeous, ridiculously expensive, hopelessly impractical, nomadic and ethereal. My instructions to Rosie, the talented young designer who fitted it out for me, were simple enough. "Think Parisian chic meets gay nightclub." Since she had never been to a gay nightclub, I had to help her out with some more specific imagery, starting with my Pinterest account, neatly arranged colour by colour and betraying my two principal interests: shoes and men. The men were supposedly there to show off their hair, styled by

Juan, but were actually there because I thought about men all of the time.

I have never really seen myself as gay; I just have this passion for men. As a teenager my mother sent me to Los Angeles to stay with my uncle so that I could improve my English and learn hairdressing. He had a successful salon in Santa Monica, where I worked twelve hours a day, six days a week, fetching coffee, sweeping the floor, fitting gowns and washing hair. My uncle asked his top stylist, Marco, to look after me and show me Los Angeles. Marco was an all-in sort of guy, and before long I was shadowing him by day and sleeping with him by night. Marco was a rock star hair stylist with A-list clients who adored him, taking me to house parties, boat parties, gallery openings, restaurants and clubs. We were living on coffee and cocaine, supplied by one of Marco's Mexican friends, our salon wages untouched since Marco knew how to live on other people's generosity. So long as we were young and beautiful, engaging and full of energy, the invitations would continue to roll in. We would never have to queue to enter a club, buy a drink in a bar or settle a restaurant bill.

I found myself covering for Marco more and more. He had moved on from party drugs to LSD, spending his days off cocooned in the bathroom shooting up, lost in psychedelia. His social circle narrowed to a handful of weirdos and male prostitutes; his working hours grew increasingly random; and our sex life became dysfunctional. He was always a creative genius at work, but his clients became fed up with his random behaviour – he turned up at work dishevelled and stinking of drugs, and I found myself looking after his A-list clients.

One evening when I was working on a fashion show, I took a call from Daniel, an African-American porn star, breathless from tantric sex and scared out of his wits. "Hey, dude, run home, Marco is in a bad way." He hung up. I took a taxi across the city, frantically calling Marco's unanswered phone. I found him naked, lying in the hallway, still breathing but only just, blood oozing out of his mouth, upstairs the paraphernalia of tantric sex. He lost consciousness and never came round. The emergency team told me he had fallen from the landing. The coroner's verdict was death by misadventure. Daniel went to ground.

The day after Marco's funeral I booked a one-way ticket to Paris, vowing never to return. I tapped a client for an attic apartment on the Île Saint-Louis, working six days a week in a salon off Boulevard Saint-Germain, spending the evenings walking alone along the Seine, visiting galleries, or going to the cinema to improve my French. For more than six months I lived like a monk, became a vegan, practised yoga and meditation to clear my mind and my body from the toxicity of Los Angeles. It was Bruno who redeemed me. A young stylist who worked alongside me at the Saint-Germain salon, he shared my interest in yoga, and we started practising together. We discussed music and philosophy well into the night and soon became inseparable, Bruno moving in with me on Saint-Louis.

The route to hair stylist rock star status was through the fashion shows, and we begged the leading stylists to let us work for them as runners for free. We basically became their slaves, washing hair, sweeping floors, arranging props for photo shoots. It was tough work, but it gave us invaluable access to the models, the stylists, the shows and the after-parties. We must have worked twenty-hour days during fashion week, but we met some amazing people. Our big break came when Catherine Solange insisted that we accompany her from show to show as her personal assistants. It was our access-all-areas pass for the fashion circus, taking us from Paris to London, Milan, New York and Miami.

Catherine has a villa on the party island of Ibiza, where she invited Bruno and me to chill between fashion shows. To us, it was idyllic. Each day started with gentle yoga on the terrace, a swim in our rooftop pool, brunch prepared by the amazing chef Mateo and served by Fernando, who seemed to know the front-of-house staff at all of the best restaurants, clubs and bars. In the afternoons we would persuade Fernando to take us bay-hopping on Catherine's motor launch, a gift from a grateful fashion house, before drinks on the beach, which inevitably turned into a beach party. Seemingly every beach bar had a club-grade mixing deck and sound system. We would usually continue the party at Catherine's villa, chilling on the pool terrace until morning, surrounded by gorgeous people. We started to get a reputation for attracting the sassiest partygoers to our late-night villa parties, which became part of the Ibiza scene.

Things got out of hand when Fernando's friends turned up with a plentiful supply of cocaine, and Catherine was unhappy that the villa was getting a reputation for free drugs and wild sex. Our idyll so nearly turned to tragedy when Daniel, scion to a Spanish banking family, was found floating face down and naked in the swimming pool, in the middle of the night. He was lucky, since Catherine's security team were patrolling the pool area, and they revived him. For me, it was time to wake up and smell the coffee. My party days were over.

CHAPTER THREE

CARLOS

I rarely admit to being a private detective. It's not so much fear of blowing my cover, it's more of an image problem. Most people's image of a private detective is a rather sad figure snooping around dustbins chasing evidence of infidelity, or stuck in a grimy office on Balham High Street surfing the nether reaches of the internet. By contrast, I like to compare myself to a high-end knee surgeon at the top of his game. My starting price is $100,000 and I rarely take on more than six assignments a year. I do some specialist corporate work but most of my clients are uber-wealthy private clients. I am the best at what I do; I usually work alone; and I enjoy the rewards. I have spent most of my life in hotels, and the *Elysium* enables me to depressurise between assignments in a secure and comfortable setting. I share the apartment with my personal trainer, Dimple, a former secret agent and the only person who has my unconditional trust.

My last assignment was the most difficult and the most lucrative of my life. Catalina Alcarez, a Spanish heiress living in London, contacted me through her private office to investigate Jimbarang Capital, a discreet hedge fund firm, where she had tens of millions invested. It wasn't the financial performance she was worried about. In fact, Jimbarang had regularly reported more than twenty per cent annualised returns for its investors. She was worried about her reputation. Her driver had overheard a cleaner speaking on a mobile phone when he was waiting for Catalina in the garage below their offices at 145 Curzon Street. "If that obnoxious man shouts at me one more time, I am going to tell Ibu Sintra about the prostitutes." Maria, the Filipino housekeeper, thought that she was alone in the garage, dropping off the laundry ready for collection that evening, and hadn't seen Bruno napping in the darkened car. Eager to pass on the whiff of scandal, Bruno related the overheard conversation to Catalina when he drove her back to her Belgravia office from Curzon Street. Catalina wasn't interested in gossip, but she was ultra-sensitive to any hint of a scandal which could corrode her family name.

There were no half-measures with Catalina. Her instructions to me were simple. "I want you to find out if I need to lose any sleep about Jimbarang Capital. Leave no stone unturned. This is between you, me and my private office. Let's meet back here in four weeks' time. Abigail, my Chief of Staff, will brief you." With that, she left me with Abigail in an elegant oval-shaped meeting room overlooking Belgrave Square. Abigail was armed with a thick due diligence report, prepared some two years previously by the private office lawyers, when Catalina had originally invested in Jimbarang. The report included background checks on Jimbarang's owners, the Sintra family and their top management. The Sintras were comfortably in the top ten most wealthy Indonesian families, having made their fortune in palm oil, and Jimbarang was originally their own family office. It was formed in 2001, when the two eldest sons, Indra and Eyo, both in their mid-twenties, were sent to London to manage the family's private investments. The brothers had both been educated in England and quickly developed an impressive black book of contacts amongst Mayfair's hedge fund community. They led discreet private lives, both married, entertaining family, friends and business contacts at the family home in Lyall Street, or their weekend retreat in the Cotswolds. The business soon expanded to include a ship-chartering operation for the family palm oil business, run by a formidable shipbroker called Mac. The brothers started co-investing alongside family friends, and within a few years they opened their own funds to investment from four other wealthy families, including the Alcarez family. From what I could see in the lawyer's report, they were smart, highly driven and extremely successful. Catalina had more than doubled her money in five years, after paying annual management fees at two per cent of funds invested and performance fees of twenty per cent of investment returns.

The lawyers' report had a lengthy section on cyber security, and one look at the spec of the systems installed at Curzon Street told me that the IT infrastructure was military grade. All staff were vetted by corporate investigators, and access within the building was controlled by iris scanners. Apparently, the lawyers were impressed when told that the brothers had originally ordered fingerprint scanners, but they had upgraded to iris scanners when they realised that fingers can be chopped off. Heads are more difficult to remove and not something to worry about if it happens to you.

Abigail had visited 145 Curzon Street several times for meetings with the Sintra brothers, and I asked her to describe the office. It was a typical Mayfair townhouse, with elegant meeting rooms on the ground floor, adorned with Indonesian sculpture. Visitors were greeted at the marble-floored entrance hall by Charles, who had swapped the peacock dress coat of a club doorman for the grey suit of a hedge fund receptionist. He was on first-name terms with all of the clients and probably kept a black book of their personal life. He always asked after Abigail's children and could book the best table at any of the top West End restaurants.

Dimple and I took it in turns to watch the office entrance from the coffee shop opposite 145 Curzon Street. The Filipino housekeeper would arrive by 6am, let herself into the front door using the iris scanner and finish her shift by noon. Charles had rooms on the top floor, leaving the building in the evenings to go to The Palmerston pub, just around the corner. The staff all arrived by car, driving directly into the underground garage, the Sintra brothers by chauffeur-driven Range Rover. There were very few visitors.

Dimple followed the Filipino housekeeper to her basement apartment in Pimlico, where she was living alone, in some poverty. Charles, by contrast, clearly had money, which he would lavish on his many friends working in the restaurants, bars and clubs of the West End. After drinks at The Palmerston, he would often go on to a late-night bar or casino, before returning to 145 Curzon Street in the early hours, high on alcohol and party drugs. It didn't take me long to realise that he was running a network of prostitutes, and it was presumably Charles who was finding girls for Eyo Sintra.

Dimple started frequenting The Palmerston, under the cover story that she had recently arrived in London and was working as a protection officer for a wealthy family in Mayfair. It didn't take long for Charles to notice Dimple, her Nepalese good looks and engaging eyes suggesting that Dimple was a party girl. I heard the conversation over the earpiece which we both wore for surveillance operations. "I heard you are a new girl on the security scene in London," purred Charles. "I am in security too, and welcome to Mayfair." By closing time they had both downed several drinks, swapping war stories about the glamorous side of private security. "Have you ever been to the Eden Club? I used to work there, and I can get us in for a late-night drink if you are interested. Just one, I promise!"

Dimple didn't take much persuading and happily succumbed to the Eden's warm embrace. She recounted the original Matisse in the lobby, the opulence of the ladies' room and the soft sophistication of drinking old fashioned cocktails in the Members' Bar. By 2am Charles was getting messy, super relaxed on his usual combination of cocaine and alcohol. "I have an apartment around the corner – why don't we chill out there for a while?" Dimple was peerless at this game, drinking just enough to encourage Charles but staying alert and sober.

Charles weaved his way along Curzon Street, telling his new friend, "You won't believe the view from my rooftop apartment." Before long Charles was pressing a glass of whisky and a cannabis joint into Dimple's hand as they stood on the balcony overlooking Green Park. Relaxed by the cannabis, Charles made his move on Dimple, running his hand over her cheekbone, telling her she was irresistible, lingering over her breasts. Dimple played along, letting Charles come on to her.

Within a few minutes Charles passed out, snoring heavily. Dimple tiptoed out of the apartment, switched back into operations mode and pulled out her iPhone. As she worked her way down the stairs she filmed every floor, taking care to avoid triggering any alarms. I met her in my Range Rover, just around the corner, and drove fast through the empty streets to our hotel in Marylebone, teasing Dimple all the way about her skill in bed.

Whilst Dimple slept off the effects of alcohol, drugs and Charles's grinding, I examined the video footage. The first two floors were very high-end offices, as you would expect from a Mayfair hedge fund, open-plan with glass desks, leather chairs, sophisticated IT, original artwork and no clutter. It was the third floor which intrigued me. The floorspace was about half of the other floors and there were no windows on the southern side, yet the building was a square-shaped townhouse. I knew from the external photos that there were windows on the third floor of the southern elevation. Why would a building yielding more than £150 per square foot in the heart of Mayfair have void space on the third floor? There was no access to the void from the rest of the third floor. Noticing that there were two elevator doors in the garage, but only one on the other floors, I realised that the second elevator connected the garage and the void on the third floor. I knew I was onto something and commissioned a drone survey later that day.

The drone operators knew their trade and sent me high-resolution video footage later that evening. I could see the void was furnished in the same style as the rest of the office, but there were only two desks and a wall of servers. Just after 9am I could make out the figure of Mac, then later in the day Eyo Sintra. Both of them spent nearly two hours on the telephone and in front of their screens. Charles appeared momentarily, delivering some packages.

I talked it through with Dimple and we concluded that Charles was our most likely source for more information on what was really going on inside the void. We knew he was running an illegal ring of prostitutes, he had probably accumulated enormous debts from living well above his means, and his life of alcohol, drugs and sex made him susceptible to blackmail. Better still, Dimple was pretty sure that she hadn't blown her cover, and Charles would be embarrassed for passing out on Dimple. Our plan was for Dimple to lead him on, get him high and aroused, then hack his phone.

Dimple's next evening with Charles followed the same pattern as the first. This time instead of the Eden Club they ended up in a private members' club off Mount Street.

Entering through an anonymous black door, they were shown to a discreet bar staffed by good-looking guys. The clientele was a mix of less good-looking but well-heeled hedgies, city types and party girls. Dimple realised that this was a pick-up joint, probably the centre of Charles's prostitute ring. They took a table next to a group of well-dressed thirty-somethings. Listening into my earpiece, I found their conversation amusing. "You were on fire last week – let's carry on from where we finished off," said Dimple, searching for any sign that her cover was blown.

"I am sorry I overplayed the weed; I can't party like I used to now I am working full-time," replied Charles. "Let's have one more whisky here, then head back to Curzon Street and play. Do you like the look of the guy at the bar, since I can ask him to join us later?" One whisky turned into two, before they weaved their way back to 145 Curzon Street. Dimple had to endure nearly an hour of Charles's foreplay before he predictably passed out, naked on the bathroom floor. Dimple swiftly found Charles's phone in his jacket in the hallway, fitted a second sim card, replaced the phone and left the apartment.

We sped back to the hotel in Marylebone, to meet Jake, a twenty-five-year-old hacker from Hong Kong who was already reading Charles's phone log. Within about twenty minutes, he had penetrated the Jimbarang Capital IT systems and, using the system architecture plans from the lawyers' due diligence report, breached the firewall into the secondary servers on the third floor. We now had phone records, voice recordings and financial data going back several years.

The three of us began the long process of forensic analysis, slowly building a complete picture of what was really happening on the third floor of 145 Curzon Street. We transformed our hotel room into a war room, complete with whiteboards recording the key people, major transactions and counterparties. By the end of day two we realised that Mac's ship-chartering operation was about much more than shipping palm oil from the Sintra family's palm oil business in Indonesia. On the surface, the financial trail looked innocent enough. There were bills of lading detailing large shipments of palm oil from the refineries in Jakarta to Rotterdam, but something didn't add up. In the previous year, the value of Mac's shipments was about ten times the value of the Netherlands' entire national palm oil imports. They had to be shipping something else and creating a paper trail to cover their tracks. Furthermore, three of the top ten buyers were companies which no longer existed on the Dutch corporate register. Jake tried some searches against the text records and struck gold with a search for *snow coke*, common slang for crack cocaine. By now we suspected that the Sintras were refining crack cocaine alongside their legitimate palm oil business, and through a laborious process of matching the phone records, voice recordings and financial transactions around the dates of the *snow coke* texts, we worked out that the Sintras were chartering ships to carry two cargoes between Jakarta and Rotterdam, their legitimate palm oil trades and a hugely profitable narcotics operation.

Armed with the chartering schedule, and list of suspect transactions, we took a flight to Amsterdam to get hard evidence. The import agents were not particularly interested in talking to us, citing privacy of contracts, but no doubt motivated by their desire to retain the Sintras' account. Edwin, a former police officer who had worked with me before, confirmed that three of the buyers listed in the transactions report were non-existent, the businesses having been dissolved some time ago. He identified a further spurious buyer, listed at a residential address. When he visited the address, the immigrant family occupying the property had never heard of the Sintras' palm oil trading company and had never been involved in the palm oil business.

We knew that the next Sintra ship was due to arrive on Saturday evening, and we monitored her progress towards Rotterdam using satellite tracking. When she was about three miles offshore, a smaller and much faster craft approached, drew alongside, and headed north towards the Noordzeekanaal. The fast boat's business could have been entirely innocent, but we suspected illicit cargo, probably narcotics, was offloaded before the ship entered the port, then spirited away into the Dutch waterways. We searched previous Sintra ship arrivals, and sure enough, the pattern was the same, the fast boat meeting the ship offshore and returning to the Seaport Marina at the western approach to the Noordzeekanaal. The satellite record gave us the fast boat's call sign, and it was easy enough for Edwin to identify her name, *Seabird*, registered in Amsterdam and moored in the Seaport Marina. She had won a Dutch powerboat race and had recently been purchased by Thomas Haase, who lived near the Prinsengracht in Amsterdam.

Haase had no presence on social media, but Edwin ran some checks and found that he was aged fifty-two, unmarried, educated in Amsterdam and had a successful career as a commodities trader in Singapore. Since returning to the Netherlands he had set up a small consultancy business which he ran from his upscale canal-side home in Amsterdam. He had no criminal record, although there were a few run-ins with the Dutch tax authorities. Clearly very wealthy, his assets included the house in Amsterdam, an extensive art collection, an apartment in Singapore, a yacht moored at Port Grimaud and the powerboat moored in the Seaport Marina. Dimple and I found a coffee shop close to the house and settled into our familiar routine of taking it in turns to watch the front door of the house. Haase lived alone in some comfort, leaving the house only for the occasional business meeting in town, daily workouts at an upmarket gym and frequent dinners with business contacts at some of Amsterdam's finest restaurants.

The gym marketing team were more than happy to sign up Dimple on a twelve-month contract, showing her the array of cardiac exercise equipment, split-level free-weights area, spa, yoga and Pilates rooms. Dimple inserted a second sim card into Haase's phone whilst he was in a yoga class and immediately left the building, never to return, hence becoming one of the gym's most profitable clients.

Haase's phone was our Pandora's box. Within a few hours we had details of every Sintra cocaine shipment, amounts wired to the front companies used by Sintra to look like buyers of legitimate palm oil and payments to Mac's personal account in Liechtenstein.

Catalina Alcarez and Abigail sat in silence as we laid out the evidence for them in Catalina's oval-shaped meeting room overlooking Belgrave Square. By 9am the following morning she was repaid her investment in full. Two minutes later, Dimple hand-delivered some data files to a financial journalist. The journalist had her scoop, brilliantly laid out in a rolling story over several weeks. The Financial Conduct Authority and the police took a little longer, eventually raiding 145 Curzon Street and arresting the Sintras and Mac. Charles is still plying his trade in Mayfair.

CHAPTER FOUR

LILY

I have a vivid childhood memory from the day the British left Hong Kong. My parents took me and my twin sister Jasmine to the waterfront to watch the *Britannia* sail out of Hong Kong harbour on the day of the handover. I didn't really understand the emotion of the handover, accentuated by the torrential rain, but I did ask my parents why they were crying. My mother's reply was confusing. "My tears are both happy and sad. My happy tears are proud that Hong Kong is returning to the Motherland, free of its colonial masters. My sad tears are saying goodbye to my British friends, and they are worried about our future."

I wanted to comfort my mother. "Don't be sad, Mama, it will stop raining soon and we can eat red bean soup." Ever since, whenever there has been a sad moment in our lives, we have gone home to eat red bean soup and comfort each other.

I have eaten quite a lot of red bean soup. There was the day Jasmine nearly drowned, getting stuck in a fisherman's net when swimming off Lamma Island, the day my first boyfriend left Hong Kong to go and live in Vancouver and the day I lost serious money on a dumb real estate trade. But there have also been a lot of tears of joy. There was the day my sister held her first art exhibition, the day I fell in love with William, a bond trader, and the day our divorce papers came through.

I bought an apartment on *Elysium* because I needed to escape. I was burned out by my job as a high-pressure real estate agent; I was burned out by love when William cheated on me; and I needed to escape and think. In a way, it's like a very expensive bowl of red bean soup.

I met William in the summer of 2008 on the very first day of our internship at the bank, on the thirty-second floor of the International Finance Centre in Central. Little did we know that we were about to have a ringside seat for the global financial crisis, in the run-up to the collapse of Lehman Brothers in September 2008.

We were both assigned to one of the bank's trading desks, buying and selling derivatives on behalf of clients. Once an obscure backwater of trading, designed to help commodities traders hedge their market risks, the desk was thrust into the limelight when commodities boomed in the run-up to the global financial crisis. Now the markets were going into freefall, and the amounts at stake were frightening. Those counterparties on the right side of the contracts were looking at profits running into tens, even hundreds of millions. Likewise, those on the wrong side were haemorrhaging losses. The problem was that the losses were so extraordinarily large that the creditors couldn't even meet their margin calls; they were declaring bankruptcy or contesting the contracts, leaving the trade unsettled and choking up the markets.

Our desk head, Wendy, had the poisoned chalice of leading the bank's relationship with Oriental Commodities Futures Limited, a top-dollar trader in derivatives, now staring at more than $100 million of losses. She took me to meet Miss Alice, the owner of Oriental, in her suite at the Lexington Hotel in Hong Kong. Miss Alice, known as the Commodities Queen, had made her name trading metals and was thought to be well-connected in Beijing. Originally set up to support her metals trading, Oriental had mushroomed into a huge derivatives house, trading across oil, metals, coal and freight derivatives. I thought that Oriental would have a sophisticated trading operation, much like the bank's own trading desks, supported by analysts and researchers. On the short walk through the IFC mall on the way to the Lexington, Wendy corrected me, telling me, "Miss Alice is an old-school trader, following her gut instinct, and most of her success has come from audacious trades against the market consensus. Miss Alice calls the shots, and her back-office staff, Molly and Kitty, execute the trades from a small office on Kowloon side and deal with margin calls and settlement. The bank thinks she is worth over $300 million, or rather she was, before the markets turned against her."

When we arrived at the hotel reception, the concierge announced, rather officiously, "Miss Alice checked out of the hotel this morning, and I believe she has urgent business in Beijing. Our driver took her to the Shenzen border crossing."

Wendy, looking increasingly alarmed, made a call to her mobile. Number unobtainable. She called Molly and Kitty in the back office and got an answerphone in English and Cantonese: "Our offices are temporarily closed – thank you for calling."

Wendy's trader's brain moved into overdrive. "The baseline scenario here is that she has done a runner, knowing that the music has stopped. The worst-case scenario is that she has upset someone in Beijing and been spirited away across the border. The best-case scenario is that she is just clearing her head on a beach in Thailand and the closure really is temporary. My gut tells me to go long on the worst-case scenario." I didn't really ease her anxiety when I reminded her that the concierge told us that Miss Alice had been driven to the Shenzen border crossing. "That points to our worst-case scenario."

Wendy returned to the IFC tower to work out how to minimise the bank's exposure before Miss Alice's disappearance became widely known across the markets. She sent me across the harbour by MTR to check out Oriental's back office on Kowloon side. It was relatively easy to find Oriental's non-descript office on Haiphong Road, above a noodle bar, nestled between the glitz of the Canton Road and the grime of Nathan Road. A young Hong Kong police officer stood guard at the door. Explaining in Cantonese that I had business with Oriental, he gave me a curt response in English. "The office is closed for security reason." He was unwilling to say any more. I called Wendy, who was busy trying to close out the bank's positions before the markets picked up on the story, leaving a voicemail message. Whilst I was in the area, I thought I may as well ask around to see if anyone knew anything about Molly and Kitty, so I asked the guy serving in the noodle bar. He knew them but didn't know where they were, explaining that they usually called by the noodle bar early in the morning, after tai chi in Kowloon Park.

I have never really done early mornings, but I was intrigued to find out more about Molly and Kitty, so I joined Master Chiu's tai chi class in Kowloon Park shortly after dawn the next morning. Strikingly handsome and strict, yet emotionally intelligent, Master Chiu had a strong following of twenty-something girls happy to learn the thirteen powers of tai chi. From a quick analysis of my fellow pupils, I think about a third were enjoying the spirituality; a third were there to express their cultural identity; and a third were there to work on their legs. A subsection of the second and third groups, both men and women, seemed more interested in Master Chiu than in tai chi. It wasn't difficult to identify Molly and Kitty, since the bank had their passport photographs on file. I knew that they would blank me if I said I was from the bank, so I tried to first gain their confidence. "That was my first-ever tai chi lesson and I found Master Chiu very strict. Is it just me?"

Molly reassured me. "He might come across as brutal but he's only teasing. Once he's sure you are serious, he will really help you to learn the thirteen powers. Why don't you join us for breakfast and we will explain more about Master Chiu's class."

At breakfast Kitty began to open up. "Master Chiu has really helped us feel stronger physically and emotionally. Molly and I had a wonderful job in finance working for a strong and powerful woman, and Master Chiu's tai chi helped us to absorb her negative energy. Things turned bad for us when the police raided our office last weekend, and Master Chiu was there to help us control a very stressful situation. The police told us Miss Alice has done something bad and warned us never to come near the office again. Miss Alice has disappeared, and we have been kicked out onto the street, but tai chi has taught us to stay calm. We know that there will always be another job in Hong Kong." I was impressed by their positivity – I promised to see them again at Master Chiu's class, made my excuses and left for work.

I was surprised when Wendy scolded me. "Lily, you really shouldn't have done that without talking to me first. I know that you meant well, but the bank's compliance guys will go mad if they ever find out. We have managed to reduce some of the bank's exposure, but we are still staring at losses in tens of millions. The markets have now picked up on Miss Alice's disappearance, crystallising our losses, and I expect the weirdos from risk management will be all over us in a matter of minutes." She was right about the weirdos who swooped onto our desk before noon that day. Wendy, who was after all the hero of the day, and had saved the bank millions, was marched out of the office by security, never to be seen again. William and I were told to take instructions only from one of the weirdos, who was installed as Caretaker Desk Manager.

Caretaker Manager turned out to be a ruthless despot and control freak, more interested in asserting his authority than restoring the desk to profitability. He enjoyed shouting at people in public, liked to control every aspect of our life and had bad breath. Within weeks, most of our colleagues had applied for a desk transfer or resigned from the bank. William and I were demoralised and disenchanted. Our despair drew us closer together, fighting the common enemy. He started taking me to the gym at lunchtime, and I started taking him to Master Chiu's early morning tai chi classes, where we became close friends with Molly and Kitty. We spent long nights together in the karaoke bars of Causeway Bay and weekends in Macau playing the roulette tables, eating sardines and drinking on the beach. When we first went to Macau, we booked separate rooms; by the second weekend I was sleeping with William, Molly with Kitty. By the third weekend we were all sleeping in the same room.

Our last day on the desk with Caretaker Manager felt like the last day of school. We were about to get our freedom back. Much to everyone's surprise, William was called by our counsellor and offered a permanent job at the bank. Unsurprisingly, I didn't get a call. We celebrated long and hard over the weekend with Molly and Kitty in Macau. Whilst we had planned a boat trip, we spent most of the weekend gossiping and snacking, smoking weed and drinking champagne out of the bottle in our hotel room. As the weed and alcohol kicked in, our conversation got wilder and wilder. I think at one stage we dared each other to think of more and more extreme ways to torture Caretaker Manager. These varied from hoax voicemails summoning him to see the compliance weirdos to delivering sex toys to his desk. Molly won when she suggested bombarding his email inbox with hoax messages from rent boys. I can vaguely remember moving on to strip poker, but my next clear memory was waking up together in the same bed.

That morning we had our first serious conversation of the weekend. Molly, still naked in bed, drew on a cigarette and put on her serious face. "William has his dream job offer. You, me and Kitty are still looking for work. But we are crazy even thinking about getting stuck on the salaryman treadmill. Most of our friends are making money in real estate. Let's do something stupid and set up our own business. Kitty and I have the connections; you have the energy. We can find the sponsors to put up the capital."

William, the smartest of all of us, encouraged us to take the risk. "I really don't want you looking back in ten years' time and regretting a missed opportunity."

And so, Bella Vista Real Estate (HK) Limited was born, taking its name from the ageing but stylish hotel where we were staying in Macau. We tapped into our girl power credentials, fast becoming the go-to residential real estate agent for new condominium developments in Hong Kong. Each time the Hong Kong government sold land for development through land sale tenders, we would work on the bidders to get appointed as selling agents. The developers knew that girl power worked for selling condos, and we were soon winning just as many appointments as the big boys. Most of our clients were speculators, buying the condo off-plan and selling on completion of the development. With Hong Kong consistently ranked number one in the global ranking of residential real estate prices per square foot, the stakes were huge, and in a rising market the profits were obscene. As our reputation grew, Bella Vista started to buy premium condos off-plan in its own name, enabling us to offer selected clients an exclusive buying opportunity, much like a wine merchant buys and sells en primeur wine. Membership of the Bella Vista Property Investors Club became a highly prized status symbol across Asia, giving us immediate access to eager investors. In order to qualify for membership, an investor had to be a woman with a net worth exceeding HK$10 million. We introduced a complex algorithm to reward bonus points for property purchases and sales and issued Gold, Black and Jade cards to members reaching each tier. Bonus points could be redeemed for exclusive spa treatments, discounts in boutiques, flights and hotel stays. We even introduced a Jade Card Townhouse, conveniently located next to the fashion boutiques in Pacific Place, for the exclusive use of Jade Card holders. It became the hottest ticket in town, always full of immaculately dressed, elegant women flaunting their status.

I was meeting one of those elegant women in the Townhouse, poring over a glossy brochure about an exciting new development on Lantau Island, when a WeChat notification flashed across my phone. It was from a girlfriend and the message started: *I have just seen William with a prostitute...*

My mind span and my heart raced as I continued the conversation with my client, telling myself not to look at my phone, trying to appear calm and engaged. Somehow, I managed to close the sale – I ran to the bathroom, locked the door and pulled out my phone. *I have just seen William with a prostitute in the Kimberley hotel. Take him to the cleaners. Men are so disgusting.* There was a picture of William emerging from a hotel lift with a glamour girl on his arm. She looked about eighteen.

I played it cool with William that evening, acting as though nothing had happened, although I had two bowls of red bean soup. I made an excuse to go to bed early, claiming that I had an important early morning meeting the next day. When he came to bed, I thought about jumping on him, bringing him close to climax then biting his cock, but in that moment, I found him disgusting. Instead, I waited until he was in a deep sleep, then crept out of bed and tiptoed into the study, where our phones were sitting on their charging stands. Working silently in the dark, so that I would not disturb William, I connected his phone to a simple storage device which I had bought from a Fortress store that afternoon. Frustratingly, it took me more than thirty minutes to download a backup, but William was still sleeping soundly when I returned to the bedroom and climbed into bed next to him.

The backup was horrifying. It felt like he didn't care since he hadn't even bothered to clear his search history, nor delete his WeChat messages. The evidence was incontestable. It had all started in the early summer, when he was searching for late-night massage spas in Wan Chai.

His credit card bills showed that he was going there at least twice a week. By late summer he had hooked up with an escort girl, taking her to romantic restaurants in Hong Kong, then on to late-night drinking clubs, karaoke bars and hotels off the Nathan Road on Kowloon side. By the autumn, he had at least three escort girls on the go at the same time, taking one of them to Manila and Bangkok. His sex drive was amazing, since he was having illicit sex at least three times a week, often making love with me later that same night.

My mind was clear. I didn't want to dwell on all the lies, the late nights when he claimed to be working on a deal at the bank, or the sacrifices I had made for him. I just marched straight into the offices of the best and most expensive divorce lawyer I could find, laid out the evidence and filed for divorce. I took the next flight out of Hong Kong to the beaches of Thailand, changed my phone, then closed it down, deleted all of my social media accounts and gave myself space to think about the future.

For five days and five nights I spoke to no one, not even the chambermaids, completely closing myself off from the world. I survived on tea and red bean soup. I felt completely in control of my emotions; there were no tears and there was no anger. On the sixth day I took a one-to-one yoga class led by Mew, a qualified yoga teacher who doubled as a swimming coach. He was about the same age as the escort girl I had seen in the Kimberley Hotel picture, and he exuded serenity. It was the first time for a week that I truly cleared my mind of William. This was all about me, and Mew asked me to dedicate my practice to myself. During savasana he spoke clearly to me, without knowing what had happened with William. "Miss Lily, have the strength to let go of all the toxins in your life, all of the relationships with people who love themselves more than they love you, all of the treasure which has no meaning and all of the labour which has no true value. Namaste." Mew probably said something similar to all of his pupils, but it felt like he was talking to my heart, and his words resonated with my feelings. As I sat cross-legged, hands in prayer on my third eye, I knew exactly what road to take.

By noon the next day I had called Molly and Kitty, asking them to collect my favourite possessions from my apartment in Hong Kong and forward them to Miami, where I would be joining the *Elysium*. I also sent a text message to William. *Don't bother to get in touch.*

CHAPTER FIVE
ROXIE

The last time I was driven down the Atlantic Road, just off Brixton High Street, I was handcuffed in the back seat next to an overweight policeman with halitosis. I can't remember the official reason for my arrest, but I am very sure that I wouldn't have been arrested if I was a shy white girl. This time I was sitting in the back seat of a chauffeur-driven Mercedes, dressed in Dior, my hand on the knee of my fiancé.

I got lucky. At fifteen, I could easily have slid into the spider's web of the county lines. My mother tried very hard to give me the stable childhood which was missing from her own life, but she never found the right man to fill the void left by my father. She never told me the full story, but I worked out the highlights from the press clippings which she kept locked away in her bedside cabinet. '*Brixton Man Found Asphyxiated in His Car*' ran one headline, '*Coroner's*

Verdict Is Suicide' another. My father had built up huge gambling debts, trying to give his wife and daughter a better life. I often think about what must have been going through his tortured mind on that dark January day in 1991, when I was less than a year old. His creditors were circling, many of them violent criminals. He couldn't run; he couldn't hide; he had already tapped his friends for loans they couldn't afford. He succumbed to his own desperation. My mother never told me the story because she was ashamed. She played no part in his downfall, yet she felt dirty, disgraced, a social pariah. Our family, friends and neighbours cut us off. Five years later, when she was walking me to school, our neighbours would cross the road to avoid walking past us. The local shopkeepers refused to serve us, and all but the outsiders ignored me at school. We were outcasts.

That was before I started singing. It was my mother who bullied me to enter a talent show. Singing was her only solace, the local gospel choir her only social activity, and I guess I grew up with a backing track of gospel music, although I hadn't been to a single lesson. The talent show was rigged in favour of Jessica, a spoilt white girl whose parents sponsored the competition. In the green room, Jessica was as catty as only a catty teenager can be. "Oh, I didn't know we had to dress up as outsiders," and "Do you have a spare hairband? Oh no, silly me, braids don't need hairbands." I ignored her, but her bullying made me determined to beat her. When I was called, I was in the zone and sang some James Blunt ballads with real zeal.

When I sang the final verse of '*You're Beautiful*' I really felt like I was flying with the angels. I will never forget that feeling, the first time that I felt a wave of love from the audience. Was this really me, an outsider? Had I really just won a talent contest, and had I just ground Jessica into dust?

My journey from an outsider on the Atlantic Road in Brixton to an insider on Primrose Hill felt like swimming through shark-infested waters. There was the creepy Fat Controller who claimed he would open doors for me, get me bookings, even a record deal. It was probably true, but I wasn't prepared to sleep with him to find out. I was tipped off by Wesley, his security guy, who I knew from my time in Brixton. "Roxie, darling, the FC is well connected, but you take care. It's no coincidence that most of his clients are young and beautiful girls like you. Word has it that he uses drugs to lure girls into his bedroom." From what I remember of Wesley, he was probably the FC's dealer, but I heeded Wesley's warning and kept my distance.

Instead, I played the long game, taking regular bookings in small jazz clubs in South London. One night at The Odyssey in Blue club in Brixton I was the warm-up act for Linda Ray, a legend of the New Orleans jazz scene and a Grammy-award-winning artist. We got talking in the green room, and she saw something of her early self in me, a shy little black girl, an outcast who could sing. She took me under her wing, insisting that I join her backing vocals and telling me, "I am going to protect you and your voice from the sharks and the slime in this business." She was true to her word, taking me on her European tour to Paris, Amsterdam, Hamburg and Berlin, negotiating fees which I could only dream about, showing me who to trust and who to avoid. We practised together as a band; she got her voice coach to work on our untrained voices; she showed us how to work the audience. In Berlin we rehearsed an adaptation of Linda's first hit, '*Soul City*', as a duet for Linda and me. It didn't make the running order, but in the middle of our second set, Linda changed her mind. "Berliners, I want to dedicate our next song to Roxie, who joined our band in London. She has the voice of a Queen of the New Orleans River." She pulled me into the limelight as the band broke into the beat of '*Soul City*'. The audience went wild, and once more I felt like I was flying with the angels, living a psychedelic dream. I was in ecstasy.

The show was live-streamed across Europe and followed by an after-party in a Berlin nightclub which felt like a maelstrom of camera flashes, interviews and sweat. There was no need for alcohol, drugs or seduction – I was already high. When I woke up the next day, I thought I was waking from a dream. My dream became reality when I turned on my phone. It crashed, overwhelmed by the messages of love shooting across social media. The luggage attendant arrived with a huge bunch of lilies and a simple card from Linda. *Roxie, my darling, you have made it.*

Berlin was a life-changing moment for me, the start of a sublime journey that would see me touring with Linda across the United States. I felt like the world was at my feet – suddenly everyone wanted to meet Roxie, the British girl. My life on the road was a whirlwind of private jets, black town cars, rehearsals, live shows, late-night parties, recordings, interviews and photo shoots. I became a style icon for British fashion in the United States. We even performed at the inauguration of the first Black female president of the United States. I met Hollywood actors, models, athletes and the legends of the recording industry.

And then the trolling started. Our publicist had warned me that it would happen, how to deal with it, how to ignore it. But I couldn't. Postings like *I hear your dad turned himself blue after hearing you sing* and *Why do men hang out with you? Maybe we should ask your dad*, made my blood boil with anger. Most of all, I had to protect my mother from this vitriol. What really freaked me out was when she received a postcard through the mail of a Black man lying dead in his car. It simply said: *I didn't know Black men turned blue.* I cancelled my tour and flew back to London to be with her.

I closed my social media accounts and took my mother to a Caribbean beach where we could swathe in the comfort blanket of anonymity, but I knew that I was addicted to the adrenalin rush of live performance. Gazing up into the sky watching the aeroplanes made me realise that the high life was where I belonged. When '*Soul City*' played at the beach bar I cracked, telling my mother that I had to finish the tour out of respect for Linda. I rejoined Linda in Miami, handed the keys to my social media accounts to our PR agents and told myself that I would never look at them again.

We played the arena to a capacity crowd over the Memorial Day weekend and I reached nirvana. The crowd was chanting my name as if I was a modern-day Jesus Christ. That's when the shooting started. At first, we assumed that someone had thrown some firecrackers, no big deal, and carried on with our set. The lights went up and the noise hit us, a tsunami of gunfire, screaming, shouting and wailing alarms. The backstage security guys hauled us off-stage to the relative security of the green room, where my head was spinning in a frenzy of shock, fear, anger and helplessness. We could hear the frenzied echoes of the stampede over our heads, as the crowd rushed for the exits, the agony as innocent people were cut down by gunfire or crushed by the stampede. The green room felt like a bunker in a war zone, twenty of us shaking with fear as the gunfire sounded ever closer. We could smell the acrid smoke and the stench of death, the screams of agony. Those screams still sit in my head, the ecstasy turning into agony. Eric, two hundred and eighty pounds of sweating hulk, was lying on top of me, protecting me from the moment we all feared, the moment when the gunmen reached the green room door. "We're going to be fine, Miss Roxie – I feel it in my bones."

Eric told me that we were inside that bunker for nineteen minutes, before a crescendo of gunfire, then silence, like the climax of a fireworks display. It was a further hour before we were hustled to the safety of a Hummer, an hour of hugging perfect strangers, brought together by the terror of the night, humbled to have survived.

I haven't picked up a microphone since that Memorial Day weekend. I guess I lost the desire. Joining the *Elysium* is my way of doing rehab.

CHAPTER SIX

ALICE

I am one of the lucky ones. I was collected from the Kai Tak East Refugee Camp in Hong Kong by Sister Maria, a Catholic nun, and taken to Paris, where Brigitte and Eric, who I call Mama and Papa, promised to bring me up as a devout Catholic, a French citizen, free from the ravages of Vietnam and the deprivations of refugee status. I remember feeling cold, dressed in the second-hand cotton clothes which had been donated to the Sisters of Mercy in Hong Kong, made for the Asian heat rather than the European winter. A green metal thermos flask was strung around my neck, encrusted with the remnants of chicken noodle soup. In my pocket was a creased photograph of my real parents, whom I never knew.

My father was an artist, whose works were good enough to sell for a few thousand francs in Papa's gallery on Rue Bonaparte just north of Boulevard Saint-Germain. Papa first met my father in pre-war Saigon when my father was a struggling young artist. They grew close, and my father would regularly send Papa paintings for sale, tightly wrapped in cotton. When the paintings stopped coming, Papa asked a Vietnamese friend to find out what had happened. My father was killed trying to escape the communists, and my mother drowned in the South China Sea, leaving me an orphan, reaching the safety of Hong Kong in the arms of a teenage boat person. I am forever grateful to Mama and Papa for finding me.

Growing up as an adopted Vietnamese girl in Paris felt quite cool, particularly because most of my parents' friends were in the art market. There is a huge Vietnamese community, and I am really proud of my heritage. I only ever wanted to be an artist, in part to build on my father's legacy, but mainly because it was my destiny. Papa kept only one of my father's pictures, which he gave to me when I graduated from art school. It's a beautiful study of my mother, in pen and ink, just 30cm x 20cm, wistfully gazing out to sea. I like to think that I am my father's pupil, and I see so much of my mother's dreaminess in my own character.

True to my roots, I eschewed the elegance of the Boulevard Saint-Germain for the raw urbanity of the Place d'Italie, where I shared a *deux pièces* above a Vietnamese restaurant with three art students, Nathalie, Amelie and Max. We rented from the *chef patron*, a serendipitous arrangement with noodle soup *compris*. It was a Bohemian life of high and low art, working on our latest project around the clock, fuelled by coffee and cigarettes. We would scour the flea markets of Avenue de Choisy or Boulevard

Raspail for interesting objects which became elements of sculpture or the subjects of still-life drawings. Our landlord was perplexed to see us carry our treasure up the narrow stairs to our apartment: a Moroccan fez, a Chinese vase, a left boot, a guitar, a stuffed bear, a tennis racquet or a Polynesian drum. All of these objects have appeared in my work. Max, who is now a successful fashion photographer, has a series of black-and-white stills of Nathalie, Amelie and me, dressed and undressed, chilling in our apartment surrounded by a menagerie of stuffed animals. It was a golden time for us, at the peak of our creativity, unrestrained by the boundaries and cynicism of adult life. Our work was perhaps immature, maybe even naive, but certainly expressive and full of energy.

Max managed to blag me a job as a creative assistant, making fashion videos for a department store. I think he slept with my boss, Bruno, a deliciously camp chain-smoking creative director, straight out of central casting. The job was my passport to the runway, giving me the opportunity to work, sleep and play with beautiful people in Paris, London and Milan. The pay didn't cover much more than coffee and cigarettes, so to cover the rent I entered the dark, beautiful and secretive world of 3615SEX. The rules of the game were simple: your client typed out their sexual fantasy over Minitel, and you replied with encouraging pillow talk. I often shared the chat lines with Nathalie, Amelie and Max, and we soon became experts in telegraphic sex.

3615SEX was initially harmless fun, and great dinner party conversation, but took a dark turn when one of my clients worked out where we lived. At first, we wondered whether he was an undercover detective, a spy or simply a tramp. He sat on a bench directly opposite our apartment every day from noon to midnight, wearing a beige mackintosh, ill-fitting jeans and off-white sneakers. We christened him Columbo, after Lieutenant Columbo, the Los Angeles television cop. Aside from writing notes in a cheap black book with a broken biro, and drinking heavily from a bottle, he simply stared directly at our door, as if in contorted contemplation.

One night when we returned home in the early hours after a night in the Marais, I noticed Columbo's black book, lying on his bench, forgotten. I picked it up and started reading it in our kitchen. The book contained a long list of dates, times and notes, which we soon realised was a log of the times when we arrived home or left the building. Why was he keeping a log and how did he know our names? Max took photos of the notebook pages, and I carefully replaced the book exactly where I found it.

I showed the photos to a young policeman, but he shrugged his shoulders, telling me that no laws had been broken and there was nothing he could do about it. "Besides, we are very busy solving real crimes. We might send someone over to ask this man, the man you call Lieutenant Columbo, what he is doing."

Two weeks later, rather to our surprise, the gendarmes were true to their word. Except that they didn't just send an officer for a chat with Columbo. They sent in the Gendarmes Nationale, complete with sub-machine guns, fast cars and balaclavas. This is because they had been tipped off that Columbo was the notorious Marseille rapist, wanted for stalking, drugging and raping sixteen young prostitutes in Marseille.

We hunkered down in our apartment for a week, feeling disgusted by Columbo's depravity, scared that he got so close to us and angry that he had shattered our innocence and freedom. I discovered my feminist-self, angry that our society tolerates sexual inequality and determined to stand up for people like those sixteen young prostitutes in Marseille. Why should a prostitute be the guilty party whilst their client is innocent? Why should a woman feel she has to restrict her freedom to protect herself from men like Columbo?

CHAPTER SEVEN

THE CROUPIER

Life on board *Elysium* as a croupier in the ship's casino was a dream job for me since the pay was good – the tips even better – I got to meet some beautiful people and experience some beautiful places. True, life at sea could be monotonous, and you had to enjoy a nomadic lifestyle, but I loved my job, and I was very good at it.

I worked in the residents' casino, an exclusive club where the residents could escape the more raucous passage guests and the down-market slot machines in the general casino. There was a clear hierarchy on board, led by the A-Deck residents. They played on the A-Deck table and insisted on me as their croupier. There was a discreet brass plaque on the table saying *A-Deck residents only*, the exception to the rule being the captain. Lower-deck residents could play at any of the other tables in the residents' casino, staffed by more junior croupiers, and they were occasionally joined by senior officers. A-Deck residents had unlimited credit, whilst lower-deck residents had a house limit.

Social discrimination like this, based solely on wealth, ran across everything on board *Elysium*. The residents dined in the exclusive residents' restaurant, with its white linen tablecloths, silver service and stewards dressed in white jackets. The A-Deck residents on the A-Deck table would be served by the maître d'hôtel and the master sommelier. The lower-deck residents would be served by stewards and the junior sommelier. By contrast, the passage guests dined in the general restaurant, where there were no tablecloths, lower-grade cutlery and crockery and less good-looking stewards. The menu was identical, except that it was written in French in the residents' restaurant and English in the general restaurant. At the A-Deck table there was no menu; instead, the maître d'hôtel and the master sommelier would make recommendations of food and wine pairings. The A-Deck had its own bar and its own swimming pool, off limits to lower-deck residents and passage guests. The cabaret hall was one of the few shared spaces, although here the social divisions were starker still. The boxes were reserved for A-Deck residents, whilst the lower-deck residents had tables in the stalls. Passage guests were restricted to the balcony.

In accordance with tradition, on the day we crossed the equator at the international date line, on day ten of our first Pacific crossing, the A-Deck residents were appointed to the Court of Neptune to carry out a line-crossing ceremony. Carlos was appointed King Neptune and Roxie became Princess Amphitrite.

They conducted initiation rites for the passage guests who were crossing the equator for the first time, including head shaving, crawling on hands and knees, being swatted with a fire hose, being locked in stocks and pelted with fruit.

Carlos and Roxie clearly enjoyed their roles, egged on by their court of A-Deck residents. King Neptune decreed armbands be issued to the passengers, gold for the A-Deck residents, red for the lower-deck residents and yellow for the passage guests. The lower-deck residents were enlisted as agents of the Court of Neptune and given responsibility for a ceremonial task, such as a Head Shaving Team, a Crawling Enforcement Team, a Fire Hose Spraying Team and a Rotten Fruits Throwing Team. Lower-deck residents who had not been assigned a specific task were appointed as spies and issued with a black armband, responsible for snitching on passage guests who ducked out of the ceremonies and residents who failed to carry out their tasks with enthusiasm. The miscreants were hauled before the Court of Neptune, handcuffed, stripped and dipped in a barrel of yellow dye.

The Crawling Enforcement Team carried out their task with particular gusto, fitting a dog collar on each unfortunate yellow-banded first-timer, attaching a lead and parading them around the deck on their hands and knees. At dinner, each first-timer was treated as a dog, forced to kneel at the heel of their red-banded owner and beg for food scraps, which were served in a bowl on the floor. None of the Crawling Enforcement Team were hauled before the Court of Neptune, since the black-banded spies approved of their enthusiasm, on occasions crossing the line by slapping the yellow bands if they made too much noise.

By contrast, the Fire Hose Spraying Team were all censured by the Court of Neptune for being too lenient on the yellow-banded passage guests. One of the yellow bands escaped when they tried to pin him down, and they compounded their crime by turning their hose on a black band who ordered them to chase the fugitive passage guest. The Fire Hose Spraying Team were duly handcuffed, stripped and dunked in a barrel of yellow dye by a crowd of baying black bands.

The A-Deck residents were occasional guests at my table during the first few days of our voyage. After crossing the line, boredom set in and they all played twelve rounds of Texas poker every evening, long into the night. The light-hearted line-crossing ceremony clearly had a huge impact on the A-Deck residents – the power had gone to their heads.

The A-Deck residents had a private arrangement amongst themselves, inspired by the line-crossing ceremony, whereby the winning player was crowned King Neptune for the night and could nominate a challenge for the losing player. At first, the challenges were light-hearted, for example on day eleven, Carlos was challenged by Roxie to wear board shorts with his tuxedo. Later, the challenges were more vulgar, for example Lily was challenged to chat up a passage guest. If the loser successfully completed the challenge, he or she would win a share of the final pot.

By day twelve, the atmosphere became more tense. Furious arguments raged about whether the loser had successfully completed the challenge. The challenge was formalised by requiring the winner to write down the challenge on a used playing card, which was sealed in an envelope and given to me for safekeeping. If there was an argument, I was to open the envelope and read out the challenge so that the Court of King Neptune, formed of the remaining players, could arbitrate. I found myself reading out a challenge so that the court could decide whether Roxie had successfully completed the challenge of drunkenly snogging the captain. That was easy enough, because they asked him, and he confirmed the deed was done.

By day sixteen, the stakes were huge and the atmosphere positively febrile. Alice had by this stage grown tired of Juan, who was constantly dissing the lower-deck residents and the passage guests. She wrote her challenge to Juan on the ace of spades. "*I challenge you to lure a passage guest to your apartment, tie him down and shave him from head to toe. If you complete your challenge by midnight tomorrow, you will win a share of the final pot.*" Juan was bubbling with excitement, exacerbated by the free-flowing champagne, and boasted to his fellow A-Deck residents about his expertise in bondage and grooming. He chose as his target Alex, an Australian dreamer who had worked his way through Asia peddling drugs and was on his way to California to live the American dream.

It was easy for Juan to lure Alex to his apartment on the promise of cocktails and pure Mexican marijuana. Before long, Juan and Alex were sharing vodka martinis and weed to the beat of Astrud Gilberto, naked in Juan's Jacuzzi. Already sky high from a night in the general casino, Alex told Juan about his journey across Asia, from the wild beach parties at Kuta to the fleshpots of Pattaya and

Bangkok, from tantric sex on the beaches of Kerala to rent boys in Manila. Juan memorably responded, "You're just getting started, darling," before recounting his exploits in Santa Monica, Paris and Ibiza.

As dawn was breaking over the horizon, Juan promised to show Alex everything he knew about tantric sex, Mexican style, and led him to his enormous circular bed. Juan used four of the silk scarves from his own collection, wrapped around each limb and tied to the bed legs, securing Alex to the bed. Whether through excitement, intoxication or both, Alex passed out, enabling Juan to shave him from head to toe with professional clippers. Alex came around some time after noon, naked in a sea of blonde hair clippings. Juan served him a Bloody Mary, telling Alex that tantric sex with him was simply amazing.

On day seventeen, I sensed the temperature of the A-Deck table reaching boiling point. Roxie and Juan folded after both losing heavily, whilst Carlos, Lily and Alice were all on a winning streak. In the final round, I drew an ace, ten and three for the flop. Carlos bet $1,000, raised to $5,000 by Lily. I drew a king for the turn and an ace for the river, with the final round of bets at $10,000. At the showdown, Lily's ace and ten gave her a full house, leaving Carlos and Alice to nurse their losses.

Lily's challenge to Roxie, the first to fold, was written on the king of spades. "*I challenge you to enslave a passage guest. If you complete your challenge by midnight tomorrow, you will receive a share of the final pot.*"

Roxie accepted the challenge and chose as her slave Marcus, the youngest of the passage guests. She plied him with alcohol and bribed him with a share of the pot. Roxie was unsure exactly what a slave should do, so she consulted her fellow A-Deck residents, who by now had formed a court to specify the precise requirements of the challenge. The court ruled that for twenty-four hours the slave would be required to walk three steps behind her, wearing a collar and led by a lead. He would wash her feet, clean her floor, bathe her and sleep on the open deck, chained to her door. Neither Roxie nor Marcus were phased by the ruling, unsurprising given that there was a lot of money at stake, a share of which Roxie had pledged to Marcus.

Roxie became quite a spectacle, parading around the A-Deck with Marcus in tow, ready to comply with her every wish. She hammed up the role, commanding Marcus to squat at the table and follow her into the cabaret hall on all fours. At night she ignored his cries, leaving him to face the cold of the mid-pacific on the open deck, chained to her door. He was given scraps to eat, but only if he begged her. Nobody quite understood why Marcus continued as Roxie's slave well past the twenty-four-hour challenge. We all thought he was performing to his audience. We didn't notice the loss of appetite, the hollow eyes, the whip lines across his back, the fact that he was shaking. We just thought that he was a very good actor.

Day twenty was the day that everything changed. All the A-Deck residents were in a dark mood, and the conversation became more and more sinister as the whisky flowed. Carlos asked each resident to describe the worst moment in their life. Juan, always wanting to be the centre of attention, leapt in. "It was the day I rushed home to find my soulmate

Marco naked and lifeless on the marble floor, blood oozing out of his mouth, wreaking of drugs and rough sex. I didn't even get the chance to say goodbye. I realised that it could have been me lying there. I felt lost, as if the music stopped, as if the world turned monochrome. Every day I wake up telling myself that I could have turned him round; I could have saved his life. I feel like I have blood on my hands."

Roxie tried to soothe him. "He chose his own path, Juan, you have to let it go. I know exactly how you feel. My father took his own life when he saw no way out of his gambling debts. He was trying to make a better life for me and my mother. I still feel the stigma; I feel like an outsider, a passage guest in a world owned by the A-Deck residents. That's why I became a resident on the *Elysium*. I wanted to be an insider."

"Me too," said Alice. "I felt dirty after being stalked by a weirdo in Paris. The truth is I feel guilty, since I started it all off. I was making money on the side by running a telephone sex line for weirdos. I feel like I encouraged him."

Carlos tried to cut through the emotions. "The fact is that the world is full of weirdos, the outsiders, the underclass, the passage guests. I meet them every day on the dark side of my investigations, from prostitutes to blackmailers and drug addicts. The way I deal with them is to dehumanise them and treat them like the scum they are."

Lily agreed. "My ex cheated on me in a sordid and disgusting way. So far as I am concerned, he is a bloodless being, just like a sea creature. I would happily string him up and rip his guts out."

Alice and Roxie nodded in agreement. "And it's always the men," they exclaimed together.

I found the conversation really disturbing; it felt like they had developed a superiority complex. The artificial society of the Elysium, exacerbated by the line-crossing ceremonies, and amplified by cabin fever, had created a class structure, with the A-Deck residents as untouchables and the passage guests as the underclass. I sensed the untouchables had lost their moral compass and were out to get the passage guests as retribution for their suffering before Elysium.

At the casino table that evening, Roxie wrote her challenge on a black jack. *Find a passage guest, string him up and rip his guts out*. Just as she hoped, Lily was the losing player and she accepted the challenge, telling everyone, "That's a perfect challenge, I know a passage guest who looks just like my ex."

I didn't sleep at all in what was left of the night, listlessly thinking through the A-Deck residents' descent into schizophrenia. She wouldn't do it, would she? Really? I kept playing through the line-crossing ceremony. Back then, we all thought they were hamming up their roles in the King's Court. Carlos was already treating everyone in the underclasses with contempt. I walked my mind through the playing-card challenges, how they quickly ratcheted up from harmless fun to abuse to grievous bodily harm. I half expected to hear the screams of an innocent man in agony as he was strung from the mast that night, his guts seeping out of his torso.

The next evening was film night and the residents and guests took their seats in the cabaret hall, the captain and the A-Deck residents in their boxes, the lower-deck residents in the stalls and the passage guests on the balcony. Precisely forty-five minutes into *Lost in Translation* the film cut, and the hall descended into darkness. Five seconds later, the screen showed video footage of Lily in the darkened casino, half naked and looking like a witch, her hair mangled, her eyes dark, her face drained of all expression. She was carrying King Neptune's spear, and she spoke into the video. "Exactly one year ago today I found out that the man I adored, the man I trusted, the man I loved unconditionally, had cheated on me in the most vile and disgusting way. All men are vile disgusting creatures. This is for you – may you rot in Hell." She raised her spear, charged and impaled William, a sweet young Chinese passage guest, who was hanging lifeless from the chandelier.

The audience screamed; the lights went up; and I stared at the captain in his usual box. Ashen-faced, he appealed for calm, as the deck officers rushed out of the cabaret hall towards the casino. I stared at the A-Deck box. Front and centre of the box was Lily, smiling, elegant and demur as ever, immaculately dressed in black. Sitting next to her was young William, equally radiant in his tuxedo, looking every inch the A-list film star that he really was. They held hands and took a bow to the rapturous audience.

As the applause died down, Lily made her acceptance speech.

"Thank you, *Elysium*, you have taught me a life lesson. We are all equal; we are all human; we are all privileged to be living this chapter of our lives on this beautiful cruise ship. Today I have handed a letter to the purser signed by all of the A-Deck residents, requesting him to allocate our accounts equally to the passage guests. We call upon the captain to bring down the walls which divide our society, let us all eat at the same table, sleep in the same cabin, swim in the same pool and party together. This is the real Elysium."

This book is printed on paper from sustainable sources managed under the Forest Stewardship Council (FSC) scheme.

It has been printed in the UK to reduce transportation miles and their impact upon the environment.

For every new title that Matador publishes, we plant a tree to offset CO_2, partnering with the More Trees scheme.

For more about how Matador offsets its environmental impact, see www.troubador.co.uk/about/